# MONTY PRICE'S NIGHTMARE

# MONTY PRICE'S NIGHTMARE

## ZANE GREY

**A WHITE IVY BOOK**

A WHITE IVY BOOK

Published by Wildside Press LLC.
www.wildsidebooks.com

# CHAPTER I

'ROUND the campfires they cursed him in hearty cowboy fashion, and laid upon him the bane of their ill will. They said that Monty Price had no friend—that no foreman or rancher ever trusted him— that he never spent a dollar—that he would not keep a job—that there must be something crooked about a fellow who bunked and worked alone, who quit every few months to ride away, no one knew where, and who returned to the ranges, haggard and thin and shaky, hunting for another place.

He had been drunk somewhere, and the wonder of it was that no one in the Tonto Forest Ranges had ever seen him drink a drop. Red Lake and Gallatin and Bellville knew him, but no more of him than the ranges. He went farther afield, they said, and hinted darker things than a fling at faro or a fondness for red liquor.

But there was no rancher, no cowboy from one end of the vast range country to another who did not admit Monty Price's preeminence in those peculiar attributes of his calling. He was a magnificent rider; he had an iron and cruel hand with a horse, yet he never killed or crippled his mount; he possessed the Indian's instinct for direction; he never failed on the trail of lost stock; he could ride an outlaw and brand a wild steer and shoe a vicious mustang as bragging cowboys swore they could; and su-preme test of all he would endure, without complaint, long toilsome hours in the piercing wind and freezing sleet and blistering sun.

'I'll tell you what," said old Abe Somers, "I've ranched from the Little Big Horn to the Pecos, an' I've seen a sight of cow-punchers in my day. But Monty Price's got 'em all skinned. It shore is too bad he's onreliable—packin' off the way he does, jest when he's the boy most needed. Some mystery about Monty."

It was an old story in the Tonto—how once when Monty returned from one of his strange absences and rode in to Cass Stringer's.

Cass was the biggest rancher in those parts, and, as it happened, at the time was without a foreman and in urgent need of men. "Monty, I'll give you a job—make you foreman—double any wages you ever got—if you'll promise to stick through summer and the fall round-up." Monty made the promise, and he ran Cass' outfit as it had never been run before; and then, with the very day of the round-up at hand, he broke his word and rode away.

That hurt Monty in the Tonto country. He never got another foreman job, but it seemed he could always find some outfit that would employ him. And strangely he was always at one and the same time unwelcome and welcome. His record made him unpopular. But, on the other hand, while he was with an outfit, he made for efficiency and speed. The extra duty, the hard task, the problem with stock or tools or harness—these always fell to Monty. His most famous trick was to offer to take a comrade's night shift.

So it often happened that while the cowboys lolled round their camp fire, Monty Price, after a hard day's riding, would stand out the night guard, in rain and snow. But he always made a bargain. He sold his service. And the boys were wont to say that he put his services high.

Still they would never have grumbled at that if Monty had ever spent a dollar. He saved his money. He never bought any fancy boots or spurs or bridles or scarfs or chaps; and his cheap jeans and saddles were the jest of his companions.

Nevertheless, in spite of Monty's shortcomings, he rode in the Tonto on and off for five years before he made an enemy.

There was a cowboy named Bart Muncie who had risen to be a foreman, and who eventually went to ranching on a small scale. He acquired a range up in the forest country where grassy valleys and parks lay between the wooded hills, and here in a wild spot among the pines he built a cabin for his wife and baby. It came about that Monty went to work for Muncie, and rode for him for six months. Then, in a dry season, with Muncie short of help and with long drives to make, Monty quit in his inexplicable way and left the rancher in dire need. Muncie lost a good deal of stock that fall, and he always blamed Monty for it.

Some weeks later it chanced that Muncie was in Bellville the very day Monty returned from his latest mysterious absence. And the two met in a crowded store.

Monty appeared vastly different from the lean-jawed, keen-eyed, hard-riding cowboy of a month back. He was haggard and thin and shaky and spiritless and somber.

"See here, Monty Price," said Muncie, with stinging scorn, "I reckon you'll spare me a minute of your precious time."

"I reckon so," replied Monty.

Muncie used up more than the allotted minute in calling Monty every bad name known to the range.

"An' the worst of all you are is thet you're a liar!" concluded the rancher passionately. "I relied on you an' you failed me. You lost me a herd of stock. Put me back a year! An' for what? God only knows what! We ain't got you figgered here—not thet way. But after this trick you turned me, we all know you're not square. An' I go on record callin' you as you deserve. You're no good. You've got a streak of yellow, an' you sneak off now an' then to indulge it. An' most of all you're a liar! Now, if it ain't all so—flash your gun!"

But Monty Price did not draw.

The scorn and abuse of the cowboys might never have been, for all the effect it had on Monty. He did not see it or feel it. He found employment with a rancher named Wentworth, and went at his work in the old, inimitable manner, that was at once the admiration and despair of his fellows. He rolled out of his blankets in the gray dawn, and he was the last to roll in at night. In a week all traces of his weakened condition had vanished, and he grew strong and dark and hard, once more like iron. And then again he was up to his old tricks, more intense than ever, eager and gruff at bargaining his time, obsessed by the one idea—to make money.

To Monty the long, hot, dusty, blasting days of summer were as moments. Time flew for him. The odd jobs; the rough trails; the rides without water or food; the long stands in the cold rain; the electric storms when the lightning played around and cracked in his horse's rnane, and the uneasy herd bawled and milled—all these things that were the everlasting torment of his comrades were as nothing to Monty. He endured the smart of rope-burned wrist, the bruise and chafe and ache of limb—all the knocks and hurts of this strenuous work, and he endured them as if they were not.

And when the first pay day came and Monty tucked away a little roll of greenbacks inside his vest, and kept adding to it as one by one his comrades paid him for some bargained service—then in Monty Price's heart began the low and insistent and sweetly alluring call of the thing that had ruined him. Thereafter sleeping or waking, he lived in a dream, with that music in his heart, and the hours were fleeting.

On the mountain trails, in the noonday heat of the dusty ranges, in the dark, sultry nights with their thunderous atmosphere he was always listening to that song of his nightingale. To his comrades he seemed a silent, morose, greedy cowboy, a demon for work, with no desire for friendship, no thought of home or kin, no love of a woman or a horse or anything, except money. To Monty himself, his whole inner life grew rosier and mellower and richer as day by day his nightingale sang sweeter and louder. Every time he felt that little bundle inside his vest a warm and delicious thrill went over him. On the long rides he pressed it with his hand a hundred times to feel if it were there, to feel the substance that made possible the fulfillment of his dream. Like a slave he toiled to add to that precious treasure.

Deep planted in his soul was a passion that drove him, consumed him. It enormously magnified the importance of his little wage, of his bargaining with his fellows, of his jealous saving. It was the very life and fire of his blood— the bent of his mind—the secret of his endurance and his dream. And when he was away from the chuck wagon and the camp fire, out on the windy range or up in the pine-sloped forest, alone and free, then he was strangely happy, thoughtlessly happy, living in his dream, planning and waiting, always listening to the song of his nightingale.

And that song was a song of secret revel—far away—where he gave up to this wind of flame that burned within him—where a passionate and irresistible strain in his blood found its outlet--where wanton red lips whispered, and wanton eyes, wine dark and seductive, lured him, and wanton arms twined around him.

# CHAPTER II

The rains failed to come that summer. The gramma grass bleached on the open ranges and turned yellow up in the parks. But there was plenty of grass and water to last out the fall. It was fire the ranchers feared.

Up on the forest ridges snow was always due in November. But the dryest fall ever known in the Tonto passed into winter without rain or snow. On the open prairie the white grass waved in the wind, so dry it crinkled; and the forest ridges were tinder boxes waiting for a spark. The ranchers had all their men riding up the parks and draws and slopes after the cattle that kept working farther and farther up. The stock that strayed was wild and hard to hold. There were far too few cowboys. And it was predicted, unless luck changed the weather, that there would be serious losses.

One morning above the low, gray-stoned, and black-fringed mountain range rose clouds of thick, creamy smoke. There was fire on the other side of the mountain. But unless the wind changed and drew fire in over the pass there was no danger on that score. The wind was right; it seldom changed at that season, though sometimes it blew a gale. Still the ranchers grew more anxious. The smoke clouds rolled up and spread and hid the top of the mountain, and then lifted slow, majestic columns of white and yellow toward the sky.

\* \* \* \*

On the day that Wentworth, along with other alarmed ranchers, sent men up to fight the fire in the pass, Monty Price quit his job and rode away. He did not tell anybody. He just took his little pack and his horse, and in the confusion of the hour he rode away. For days he felt that his call might come at any moment, and finally it had come. It did not occur to him that he was quitting Wentworth at a most critical time; and it would not have made any difference to him if it had occurred to him.

He rode away with bells in his heart. He felt like a boy at the prospect of a wonderful adventure. He felt like a man who had toiled and slaved, whose ambition had been supreme, and who had reached the pinnacle where his longing would be gratified. His freedom stirred in him the ecstatic emotion of the shipwrecked mariner who from a lonely height beheld a sail, He was strained, tense, overwrought. For six months he had been chained to toil he hated. And now he was free. He was going. He was on the way. The keen wind seemed like wine. For once he saw the blue of the sky, the beauty of the bold peaks in the distance. And he pulled in his horse upon the ridge of a high foothill, where the trail forked, and looked across the ranges, away toward the south that called him.

Monty Price was still a young man. Of light but powerful build, rangy and wiry, darkly bronzed, with eyes like coals of fire, he appeared a handsome cowboy. His face was hard, set, stern, like that of all men of his kind, and there was nothing in it to suggest his failing or that he deserved the brand that Muncie had put upon him. He seemed good to look at. There was something of the open, free ranges in his look and his action.

The smell of burning pine turned Monty round to face the north. There was valley below him, then open slopes, and patches of pine, rising gently to billow darkly with the timbered mass of the mountain. A pall of smoke curled away from the crest, borne on a strong wind. The level line of smoke broke sharply at the pass and turned toward him, running down into the saddle between the bluffs. The fire in the pass was gaining. He thought grimly that all the men in the Tonto country could not check it.

"Sure she's goin' to burn over," he muttered. "An' if that wind changes-whoopee!"

His road led to the right away from the higher ground and the timber. To his left the other road wound down the ridge to the valley below and stretched on through straggling pines and clumps of cedar toward the slopes and the forests. Monty had ridden that road a thousand times. For it led to Muncie's range. And as Monty's keen eye swept on over the parks and the thin wedges of pine to the black mass to timber beyond he saw something that made him draw up with a start. Clearly defined against the blue-black swelling slope was a white-and-yellow cloud of smoke. It was moving. At thirty miles distance, that it could be seen to move at all, was proof of the great speed with which it was traveling.

"She's caught!" he ejaculated. " 'Way down on this side. An' she'll burn over. Nothin' can save the range!"

He watched, and those keen, practiced eyes made out the changing, swelling columns of smoke, the widening path, the creeping dim red.

"Reckon that'll surprise Wentworth's outfit," soliloquized Monty thoughtfully. "It doesn't surprise me none. An' Muncie, too. His cabin's up there in the valley."

It struck Monty suddenly that the wind blew hard in his face. It was sweeping straight down the valley toward him. It was bringing that fire. Swift on the wind!

"One of them sudden changes of wind!" he said. "Veered right around! An' Muncie's' range will go. An' his cabin!"

Straightway Monty grew darkly thoughtful. He had remembered seeing Muncie with Wentworth's men on the way to the pass. In fact, Muncie was the leader of this fire-fighting brigade.

"Sure he's fetched down his wife an' the baby," he muttered. "I didn't see them. But sure he must have."

Monty's sharp gaze sought the road for tracks. No fresh track showed! Muncie must have taken his family over the short-cut trail. Certainly he must have! Monty remembered Muncie's wife and child. The woman had hated him. But little Del with her dancing golden curls and her blue eyes—she had always had a ready smile for him. It came to Monty then suddenly, strangely, that little Del would have loved him if he had let her. Where was she now? Safe at Wentworth's, without a doubt. But then she might not be. Muncie had certainly no fears of fire in the direction of home, not with the wind in the north and no prospect of change. It was quite possible—it was probable that the rancher had left his family at home that morning.

Monty experienced a singular shock. It had occurred to him to ride down to Muncie's cabin and see if the woman and child had been left. And whether or not he found them there the matter

of getting back was a long chance. That wind was strong—that fire was sweeping down. How murky, red, sinister the slow-moving cloud!

"I ain't got a lot of time to decide," he said. His face turned pale and beads of sweat came out upon his brow.

That sweet little golden-haired Del, with her blue eyes and her wistful smile! Monty saw her as if she had been there. Then like lightning flashed back the thought that he was on his way to his revel. And the fires of hell burst in his veins. And more deadly sweet than any siren music rang the song of his nightingale in his heart. Neither honor nor manliness had ever stood between him and his fatal passion. Nothing, he thought, no claim of man or child or God, could stop him. No situation had ever before arisen with the power to make him even think of resisting. A million times sweeter sang his nightingale, imperiously, wonderfully. He was in a swift, golden dream, with the thick fragrance of wine, and the dark, mocking, luring eyes on him. All this that was more than life to him—to give it up—to risk it—to put it off an hour! He felt the wrenching pang of something deep hidden in his soul, beating its way up, torturing him. But it was strange and mighty. In that terrible moment it decided for him; and the smile of a child was stronger than the unquenchable and blasting fire of his heart.

# CHAPTER III

Monty untied his saddle pack and threw it aside; and then with tight-shut jaw he rode down the steep descent to the level valley. His horse was big and strong and fast. He was fresh, too, and in superb condition. Once down on the hard-packed road he broke into a run, and it took an iron arm to hold him from extending himself. Monty calculated on saving the horse for the run back. He had no doubt that would be a race with fire. And he had been in forest fires more than once.

The big bay settled into a steady, easy-running gait. The valley floor sloped up quite perceptibly, and the road was many times cut and crossed by a dry wash. Soon Monty reached the bleached and scraggy cedars—and the scant thickets of scrub oak—and then the straggling pines. They were dwarfed and gnarled, and many were dead. As he advanced, however, these trees grew thicker and larger. Then he rode out of the pines into a park, where the white grass and the gray sage waved in the wind.

A dry, odorous scent of burning wood came on the breeze. He could still see part of the smoke cloud that had alarmed him, but, presently, when he had crossed into the pines again it passed from his sight. The ascent of the valley merged into level and the slopes widened out and the road crossed park after park, all girdled by pines. Then he entered the forest proper. It was dark and shady. The great pines stood far apart, with only dead limbs low down, and high above, the green, lacy foliage massed together. There was no underbrush. Here and there a fallen monarch lay with great slabs of bark splitting off. The ground was a thick brown mat of pine needles, as dry as powder.

The dry, strong smell of pine was almost sickening. It rushed at Monty—filling his nostrils. And in the tree-tops there was a steady, even roar of wind. Monty had a thought of how that beautiful brown and green forest, with its stately pines and sunny glades, would be changed in less than an hour.

There seemed to be a blue haze veiling the aisles of the forest, and Monty kept imagining it was smoke. And he imagined the roar in the pines grew louder. It was his impatience and anxiety that made the ride seem so long. But he was immensely relieved when he reached Muncie's corral. It was full of horses, and they were snorting, stamping, heads up, facing the direction of the wind. That wind seemed stronger, more of a warm, pine-laden blast, which smelled of fire and smoke. It appeared to be full of fine dust or ashes. Monty dis-mounted and had a look at his horse. He was wet and hot, just right for a grueling race. Monty meant to let down the bars of the corral gate, so that Muncie's horses could escape, but he was deterred by the thought that he might need another mount. Then he hurried on to Muncie's cabin.

This was a structure of logs and clapboards, stand-ing in a little clearing, with the great pines towering all around. Presently Monty saw the child, little Del, playing in the yard with a dog. He called. The child heard, and being frightened ran into the cabin. The dog came bark-ing toward Monty. He was a big, savage animal, a trained watchdog. But he recognized Monty.

Hurrying forward Monty went to the open door and called Mrs. Muncie. There was no immediate response. He called again. And while he stood there waiting, listening, above the roar of the wind he heard a low, dull, thundering sound, like a waterfall in a flooded river. It sent the blood rushing back to his heart, leaving him cold. He had not a single instant to lose.

"Mrs. Muncie," he called louder. "Come out! Bring the child! It's Monty Price. There's forest fire! Hurry!"

Still he did not get an answer. Then he called little Del, with like result. He reflected that the mother often drove to town, leaving the child in care of the watchdog. Besides, usually Muncie or one of his men was near at hand. But now there did not seem to be anybody here. And that dull, continuous sound shook Monty's nerve. He yelled into the open door. Then he stepped in. There was no one in the big room—or the kitchen. He grew hurried now. The child was hiding. Finally he found her in the clothespress, and he pulled her out. She was frightened. She did not recognize him.

"Del, is your mother home?" he asked.

The child shook her head. With that Monty picked her up, along with a heavy shawl he saw, and, hurrying out, he ran down to the corral. The horses were badly frightened now. Monty set little Del down, threw the shawl into a watering trough, and then he let down the bars of the gate. The horses pounded out in a cloud of dust. Monty's horse was frightened, too, and almost broke away. There was now a growing roar on the wind. It seemed right upon him. Yet he could not see any fire or smoke. The dog came to him, whining and sniffing.

With swift hands Monty soaked the shawl thoroughly in the water, and then wrapping it round little Del and holding her tight, he mounted. The horse plunged and broke and plunged again—then leaped out straight and fast down the road. And Monty's ears seemed pierced and filled by a terrible, thundering roar.

For an instant the awful and unknown sound froze him, stiffened him in his saddle, robbed him of strength. It was the feel of the child that counteracted this and then roused the daredevil in him. The years of his range life had engendered wildness and violence, which now were to have expression in a way new to him.

He had to race with fire. He had to beat the wind of flame to the open parks. Ten miles of dry forest, like powder! Though he had never seen it he knew fire backed by heavy wind could rage through dry pine faster than a horse could run. He would fail in the one good deed of his life. And flashing into his mind came the shame and calumny that before had never affected him. It was not for such as he to have the happiness of saving a child. He had accepted a fatal chance; he had forfeited that which made life significant to attempt the impossible. Fate had given him a bitter part to play. But he swore a grim and ghastly oath that he would beat this game. The intense and abnormal passion of the man, damned for years, never controlled, burst within him— and suddenly, terribly, he awoke to a wild joy in this race with fire. He had no love of life—no fear of death. All that he wanted to do—the last thing he wanted to do was to save this child. And to do that he would have burned there in the forest and for a million years in the dark beyond.

So it was with wild joy and rage that Monty Price welcomed this race. He goaded the horse. Then he looked back.

Through the aisles of the forest he saw a strange, streaky, murky something, moving, alive, shifting up and down, never an instant the same. It must have been the wind, the heat before the fire. He seemed to see through it, but there was nothing beyond, only opaque, dim, mustering clouds. Hot puffs shot into his face. His eyes smarted and stung. His ears hurt, and were being stopped up. The deafening roar was the roar of avalanches, of maelstroms, of rushing seas, of the wreck and ruin and end of the world. It grew to be so great a roar that he no longer heard. There was only silence. His horse stretched low on a dead run; the tips of the pines were bending in the wind; and wildfire was blowing through the forest, but there was no sound.

Ahead of him, down the road, low under the spreading trees, floated swiftly some kind of a medium, like a transparent veil. It was neither smoke nor air. It carried faint pin points of light, sparks, that resembled atoms of dust floating in sunlight. It was a wave of heat propelled before the storm of fire. Monty did not feel pain, but he seemed to be drying up, parching. All was so strange and unreal—the swift flight between the pines, now growing ghostly in the dimming light—the sense of rushing, overpowering force—and yet absolute silence. But that light burden against his breast—the child—was not unreal.

He fought the desire to look back, but he could not resist it. Some horrible fascination compelled him to look. All behind had changed. A hot wind, like a blast from a furnace, blew light, stinging particles into his face. The fire was racing in the treetops, while below all was yet clear. A lashing, leaping, streaming flame engulfed the canopy of pines. It seemed white, seething, inconceivably swift, with a thousand flashing tongues. It traveled ahead of smoke. It was so thin he could see the branches through it, and the dirty, fiery clouds behind. It swept onward a sublime and an appalling spectacle. Monty could not think of what it looked like. It was fire, liberated, freed from the bowels of the earth, tremendous, devouring. This, then, was the meaning of fire. This, then, was the burning of the world.

He must have been insane, he thought, not to be overcome in spirit. But he was not. He felt loss of something, some kind of sensation he ought to have had. But he rode that race keener and better than any race he had ever before ridden. He had but to keep his saddle—to dodge the snags of the trees—to guide the maddened horse. No horse ever in the world had run so magnificent a race. He was outracing wind and fire. But he was running in terror. For miles he held that long, swift, tremendous stride without a break. He was running to his death whether he distanced the fire or not. For nothing could stop him now except a bursting heart. Already he was blind, Monty thought.

And then, it appeared to Monty, although his steed kept fleeting on faster and faster, that the wind of flame was gaining. The air was too thick to breathe. It seemed ponderous—not from above, but from behind. It had irresistible weight. It pushed Monty and his horse onward in their flight—straws on the crest of a cyclone.

Again he looked back and again the spectacle was different. There was a white and golden fury of flame above, beautiful and blinding; and below, farther back, a hellishly dark and glowing fire, black-streaked, with tumbling puffs and streams of yellow smoke, The aisles between the burning pines were smoky, murky caverns, moving, coalescing, weird, and mutable. Monty saw fire shoot from the treetops down the trunks, as if they were trains of powder; and he saw fire shoot up the trunks. They went off like huge rockets. And along the ground leaped the little flames, like oncoming waves in the surf. He gazed till his eyes burned and blurred, till all merged into a wide, pursuing storm too awful for the gaze of man.

Ahead there was light through the forest. He made out a white, open space of grass. A park! And the horse, like a demon, hurtled onward, with his smoothness of action gone, beginning to break.

A wave of wind, blasting in its heat, like a blanket of fire, rolled over Monty. He saw the lashing tongues of flame above him in the pines. The storm had caught him. It forged ahead. He was riding under a canopy of fire. Burning pine cones, like torches, dropped all around him, upon him. A terrible blank sense of weight, of agony, of suffocation—of the air turning to fire! He was drooping, withering when he flashed from the pines out into an open park. The horse broke and plunged and went down, reeking, white, in convulsions, killed on his feet. There was fire in his mane. Monty fell with him, and lay in the grass, the child in his arms. There was smoke streaming above him, and his ears seemed to wake to a terrible, receding roar. It lessened, passed away, leaving behind a crackling, snapping, ripping sound. The wind of flame had gone on. Monty lay there partially recovering. The air was clearer. Still he was dazed.

Fire in the grass—fire at his legs roused him. He experienced a stinging pain. It revived him. He got up. The park was burning over. It was enveloped in a pall of smoke. But he could see. Drawing back a fold of the wet shawl, he looked at the child. She appeared unharmed. Then he set off running away from the edge of the forest.

It was a big park, miles wide. Near the middle there was bare ground. He recognized the place, got his bearings, and made for the point where a deep ravine headed out of this park.

Beyond the bare circle there was more fire, burning sage and grass. His feet were blistered through his boots, and then it seemed he walked on red-hot coals. His clothes caught fire, and he beat it out with bare hands. Agony of thirst tortured him, and the beating, throbbing, excruciating pain of burns. He lost his way, but he kept on. And all about him was a chaos of smoke. Unendurable heat drove him back when he wandered near the edge of the pines.

Then he stumbled into the rocky ravine. Smoke and blaze above him—the rocks hot—the air suffocating—it was all unendurable. But he kept on. He knew that his strength failed as the conditions bettered. He plunged down, always saving the child when he fell. His sight grew red. Then it grew dark. All was black, or else night had come. He was losing all pain, all sense when he stumbled into water. That saved him. He stayed there. A long time passed till it was light again. His eyes had a thick film over them. Sometimes he could not see at all. But when he could, he kept on walking, on and on. He knew when he got out of the ravine. He knew where he ought to be. But the smoky gloom obscured everything. He traveled the way he thought he ought to go, and went on and on, endlessly. He did not suffer any more. The weight of the child bore him down. He rested, went on, rested again, went on again till all sense, except a dim sight, failed him. Through that, as in a dream, he saw moving figures, men looming up in the gray fog, hurrying to him.

* * * *

Far south of the Tonto Range, under the purple shadows of the Peloncillos, there lived a big-hearted rancher with whom Monty Price found a home. He did little odd jobs about the ranch that by courtesy might have been called work. He would never ride a horse again. Monty's legs were warped, his feet hobbled. He did not have free use of his hands. And seldom or never in the presence of anyone did he remove his sombrero. For there was not a hair on his head. His face was dark, almost black, with terrible scars. A burned-out, hobble-footed wreck of a cowboy! But, strangely, there were those at the ranch who learned to love him. They knew his story.

Lightning Source UK Ltd.
Milton Keynes UK
UKOW042139090413

208965UK00002B/347/P